PUFFIN

DANGER

K. M. Peyton was brought up in the London suburbs. Later her family moved north and she studied at Manchester Art School where she met her husband, now a cartoonist. After a spell of teaching and travelling abroad, they settled in Essex, where they still live today. Her joys in life are her horses, her garden, sailing and fell-walking with her husband. She has written since she was a child and has had over forty novels published, of which the best known and best loved must be the *Flambards* quartet, which won the Carnegie Medal and the *Guardian* Award.

SURFERS

Danger Offshore

K. M. Peyton

Illustrated by
Bob Harvey

PUFFIN BOOKS

For William

PUFFIN BOOKS

Published by the Penguin Group
Penguin Books Ltd, 27 Wrights Lane, London W8 5TZ, England
Penguin Putnam Inc., 375 Hudson Street, New York, New York 10014, USA
Penguin Books Australia Ltd, Ringwood, Victoria, Australia
Penguin Books Canada Ltd, 10 Alcorn Avenue, Toronto, Ontario, Canada M4V 3B2
Penguin Books (NZ) Ltd, 182–190 Wairau Road, Auckland 10, New Zealand

Penguin Books Ltd, Registered Offices: Harmondsworth, Middlesex, England

First published 1998
3 5 7 9 10 8 6 4

Text copyright © K. M. Peyton, 1998
Illustrations copyright © Bob Harvey, 1998
All rights reserved

The moral right of the author and illustrator has been asserted

Filmset in Bembo

Made and printed in England by Clays Ltd, St Ives plc

British Library Cataloguing in Publication Data
A CIP catalogue record for this book is available from the British Library

ISBN 0–140–38959–8

Contents

Contents

Chapter One
The Invitation

CORKY NORTH AND David Shine, known as Shiner, were in the same class at school. Corky was athletic, bright, and good at just about everything. He was brilliant – everyone wanted to be his friend. Amazingly he was truly nice, not the slightest bit big-headed.

Shiner had none of Corky's talents. He was reliable, steady, he tried, he was a staunch friend. Shiner was a plodder. Dull, in a word. He didn't expect to be in Corky's bright circle. But they had something in common that no one else in the class had.

They were windsurfers.

Everyone knew Corky was a windsurfer because he was in the county team. He was in the newspapers. He won silver cups. But he never boasted about it.

Nobody knew Shiner was a windsurfer because he never mentioned it. And Corky only found out because Shiner's wetsuit fell out of his locker one day when Corky was passing. Shiner was going for a lesson after school.

"Hey, Shiner, what's this for? You go sailing?"

"Surfing," Shiner muttered.

"I didn't know! Where d'you go?"

"Only on the reservoir."

"There's good surfing on the reservoir," Corky said encouragingly.

Shiner didn't say anything. He didn't want to let the cat out of the bag – that the reservoir he went to was a potty little farmer's lake, not the big waterworks one Corky thought he meant.

The farmer's son had set up a little school and taught a few hopefuls in his spare time. He had provided a caravan to change in and make cups of tea. He spent most of his time teaching his pupils how to pull themselves up when they had fallen off. Shiner had had a lot of practice at this. But lately . . . he had been staying upright, going quite fast. And thinking he was outgrowing the farmer's lake.

Everyone knew that Corky sailed on the sea. Proper stuff.

Shiner had taken his board down to the estuary a few times and tried it, but only on calm days. And he had been frightened. He had told himself there was absolutely no reason to be frightened. But he was. His instructor was always telling him he lacked confidence.

Thinking of this now, he said –
confidently – "Yeah, it's great."

After that, Corky used to talk to him
about surfing. Shiner could answer with
all the right jargon, and somehow
Corky got the idea he was good. Shiner
was sure he had never lied or boasted,
but Corky got it into his head that
Shiner was his surfing buddy.

"How about coming down to the
cottage with me at Easter? My mum
and dad stay there for a week and I surf
every day. It would be great if you could
come."

"I've never surfed out at sea!"

"You'd love it. It's fantastic after still
water."

"I'd never keep up with you."

Shiner back-pedalled fast, feeling real panic. Surfing with Corky! *At sea!* Shiner could feel himself falling off already.

"I'll get my mum to phone yours," Corky said. "It's a great place, where we go. Nothing for miles and miles."

No caravan with cups of tea. No kindly instructor saying, "All you need is confidence, Shiner." No rescue dinghy.

"Honestly, I'd just hold you up all the time!"

Too late now, to admit how useless he was. The damage was done. He tried to change the subject.

"What do your parents do all day? They're not windsurfers?" Windsurfing wasn't something parents did.

"No. My ma paints, watercolours and

6

stuff, and they both go off in the car and play golf. And they're both keen on birds. Birdwatching. They love Flatlands – you'll see – there's nothing there at all, just marshes and dunes for miles. If I didn't have surfing I'd go potty."

Corky's father was a doctor. He rang up that same evening to invite Shiner to the cottage. Shiner's parents thought it a great idea. They both worked, and worried about not being around in the school holidays.

"Such nice people the Norths, too," Shiner's mother enthused. "How kind of them to invite you! You'll have a wonderful time! Doctor North said he'll be really glad to have you along, as company for Corky."

7

"My dad thinks you'll keep me out of his hair," Corky translated. "He just wants a quiet life when we go on holiday. That's why we go to Flatlands."

And Shiner could find no excuse for refusing to go.

Chapter Two
Voices in the Night

SHINER COULD SEE what Corky meant about a quiet life.

Flatlands was great. It was a long spur of land sticking out into the sea, with just dunes and marshland and absolutely nothing to be seen except a few bullocks grazing in the distance and seabirds pecking on the shoreline. The so-called cottage was an old bungalow on a dirt lane that ran up from the nearest farm. The dirt lane went out to the furthest dunes and stopped.

"Nobody ever comes up here," Corky said. "It's like living on the moon."

But the bungalow was very comfortable and Corky's mother stocked the freezer with an enormous amount of food, which promised well. The boys had a room in the loft with a window looking out to sea, and they had computer games for when it rained and a load of CDs. Corky's father zonked out on holiday, according to Corky.

"He likes nothing happening," Corky

said. "He won't go to a place where anything happens."

Mum North had a load of tapestry and ten long novels, besides all her painting things. Weird sort of holiday, Shiner thought, thinking how his parents liked Great Yarmouth and Brighton and going round the shops and discoing at night. Here the only light was from a skyful of stars such as Shiner had never seen.

"It's all sky here," Mrs North said. "Wonderful for painting."

Well, Shiner could see that.

"We could go down to the end, if you like," Corky said to Shiner, restless after the long car journey. "What time's supper?"

"Give me an hour to get sorted."

"Come on then."

"You'll have to walk," the doctor said. "I'm not unloading the bikes till morning. They're underneath the golf clubs and all the rubbish your mother likes to bring."

"That's OK," Corky said.

Shiner did not go for walks as a rule. This holiday was certainly going to be different.

"It's nearly two miles to the beach at the end. We'll just do it," Corky said.

Shiner bit back his gasp of dismay. Four miles! And he was on *holiday*!

But it was magic outside – the sky full of stars, the lane fringed with reeds that rustled in the soft, warm breeze. Shiner's heart rose. He wasn't so awful, he told himself – just lacking confidence. His trainer at the reservoir told him he was too tense on the board – "Relax, and it will all come together." A fortnight with Corky, surfing every day, was bound to get him going. If only he didn't make a complete fool of himself . . .

"That's funny," Corky said. "A light –"

"Where?"

"It could be a boat, I suppose. At the end, where we're going. Nobody ever comes down here, only a tractor sometimes."

Shiner could see it, far away, like a car headlight.

They walked on and the light went

out. After a while Corky stopped and said, "Listen."

They listened. Shiner had never heard such silence – it was almost frightening. Only the faintest rustle in the reeds, then a bird's eerie cry far out across the water. Nothing. He shivered, and thought he heard the shiver. Then, unmistakably, on a shred of breeze, voices. They came from the end of the lane, where the light had been shining. In the still air the voices carried, just enough to be heard.

"Weird," Corky said. "Perhaps someone's landed for a barbecue."

"They're quarrelling," Shiner said.

They stood still to hear, holding their breath.

The light came on again and then an engine started up, drowning the voices. There was a car at the end, or a lorry by the sound of it. The light wavered, disappeared, came on again. The engine noise grew louder.

"Whoever can it be?" Corky said.

Whoever it was, they were in a great hurry. The engine noise grew rapidly louder and the headlight flared. It was very strange but both boys instinctively moved off the lane and into the reed bed.

"Get down," Corky said.

Afterwards, neither of them could say why they wanted to be hidden. The vehicle was a Transit van and passed at great speed, throwing up a cloud of dust. It seemed very heavily loaded, down on its springs, and thumped dangerously through the potholes. It was impossible to see the driver, only an impression of a fierce-looking man. And another on the passenger seat.

Corky and Shiner stood up and stared after it.

"Weird," Corky said again. "Madman, driving like that."

"What are they doing out here?"

"Not having a barbecue, that's for sure. Let's go and look for clues."

The rest of the walk was so lonely and quiet it was hard to believe they had seen such a disturbance. Where the lane ended there was a line of dunes. They ran up the soft sand and peered over the top. The sea spread silver in the starlight to the edges of the world, it seemed. Nobody. No light. No movement, save the softest rolling murmur of the sea lapping on the small shelly beach.

Corky slid down the far side.

"Look, a boat's been pulled up here."

There was a keel mark on the beach, fast being eaten up by the incoming tide. Also what looked like a lot of footmarks, all in a big circle, then trailing away into the dunes. In the dunes it was too dark to see where they went. But they could see the wheelmarks of the Transit van.

"They landed from a boat, lots of them," Shiner said.

"Could be fishermen, I suppose,"

Corky said dubiously. "They go out for day trips. But funny to land here."

They stood on the dunes and stared out to sea. They thought they could hear a boat engine out there. Or was it imagination?

"There's an island out there," Corky said. "Just dunes and an old shed. Can you see it?"

Shiner couldn't.

"We could go there tomorrow, if you like. It's better having a destination, instead of just zooming about."

"If the wind's light." Shiner bit down his panic. "I'm not as good as you, remember."

"Two of us – can't go wrong."

Want to bet? Shiner thought.

"I'm starving! Let's get back."

When they were hustling home along the lane, Corky said, "Whatever those guys were up to, there's no clues left now on the beach. The tide will have covered those marks up."

But Shiner had already forgotten the intruders. He was thinking about taking his board out to an offshore island. In the *sea* – with waves coming at him to tip him off balance. The board would move under his feet like crazy and he would have to keep his balance. Bad enough when the water was smooth.

But with luck the wind would come up and blow too hard.

However, in the night when he awoke he could hear a perfect pitch of breeze sighing over the roof tiles, inviting all windsurfers to come and play.

Chapter Three
To the Island

"PERFECT!" CORKY SHOUTED, turning
from the window. "Force four-ish, wind
south-westerly. Nothing to frighten you,
Shiner! Day out for beginners! Get
moving!"

Shiner would rather have turned over

and put the blanket over his head. Then he told himself, severely, he was being stupid. He wasn't *that* bad! It was all in the mind. Once they were under way he would enjoy it, for sure . . . well, perhaps . . . He groaned into the pillow.

Corky threw a trainer at him.

Then they were up and dressed, and Mum North made a huge breakfast: fried egg, bacon, baked beans and fried bread.

"For heaven's sake, don't fall in. You'll sink like stones."

Dr North said he would run them down to the beach in the car, with the boards on the roof. And the bikes in the back, to come back on. The shelly beach was the best place for taking off from, although there were places nearer the bungalow.

"But muddy," Corky said. "It's best off the dunes, where we were last night."

Strangely, neither of them mentioned the incident of the Transit van to the doctor. There was no sign of anything unusual this morning. The island, which Shiner had failed to see last night, was now visible on the horizon, very low and very small. It looked miles away! (It *was* miles away.) And, although the wind was light, wind against tide was knocking up what Shiner thought were quite big waves. Well, they looked big.

"Fine for your first go. Flat as a pancake," Corky said.

Shiner said, to make quite sure Corky

23

knew, "I've never sailed in anything but flat water."

"Really boring, flat water," Corky laughed.

He obviously didn't think it was a problem.

At least, Shiner thought, his gear was good. His wetsuit was newer than Corky's faded garment with rips in the elbows, and his board was OK. It was long and stable – a beginner's board. Corky's was a light, lean job, a short board, a little thoroughbred. To ride that you had to be pretty good.

But Corky's appraising glance saw nothing wrong. (Only the driver, thought Shiner.)

Taking off from the beach was a bit

different from the reservoir wall. It was tricky but – amazingly – he survived. Corky was ahead, up and skimming fast and not looking back. Encouraged, Shiner strived to remember all he had learnt: bodyweight to control the force on the sail . . . weight on the back foot. Shuffle, shuffle . . . the sail lurched alarmingly away from him in the sudden gust, but he didn't panic, gave to it, got it back, hit the next wave spot on and zoomed down the other side.

This was great! All of a sudden, Shiner for the first time ever felt a rush of adrenalin as his self-confidence zoomed. It was true – waves were great! Corky was miles ahead, his gaudy little sail zooming over the sea at a wild angle.

The island that had seemed so far away now seemed to beckon. A buoy bobbed in the water and Corky, creaming back towards him, shouted, "There's a sandbank there! Go left of the buoy or you might hit bottom!"

Shiner knew that all the water off Flatlands was full of dangerous shoals. That's why it was empty of ships and even yachts. Only the few fishermen knew their way about. But it seemed that even windsurfers had to know the way.

"You're doing fine!" Corky shouted.

Corky was going about three times as fast and zooming back in circles to keep in touch but Shiner's confidence increased by the minute. By the time the island was well in his sights he hadn't made a complete hash of it.

Corky went ahead and made a controlled and perfect landing up the sloping sand. Shiner, praying hard, slowed down as best he could and flapped to a standstill more or less in the right place. Fantastic! He laid the rig down and stepped off on to firm sand.

"Great place," Corky said. "It's quite big at low water, but when the tide's up there's just those dunes and that little hut."

He seemed to take it for granted that Shiner had coped.

But Shiner, overcome with relief and glowing with achievement, felt he had come to paradise. When he looked back towards shore and saw how far he'd come he was astonished. He tried to play it cool, not let on how great he felt. But his heart was smashing in his chest with pure excitement. He could not believe how easy it had turned out, after all the terrors.

"Yeah, great place." He tried to sound laid back. "What's the hut for?"

"Oh, wildfowlers, once. Nobody uses it now."

They pulled the boards up the sand and wandered along towards the hut.

It was a simple affair, made of tarred boards, open on the side nearest the sea.

"Great place to camp," Corky said.

"You'd never get the gear out here on the boards," Shiner said.

"Oh, I don't know. I think you could. Only thing is my mum and dad don't know I come out this far. They'd go spare."

Shiner felt a qualm at this remark. Corky was brilliant – didn't they know? If anyone should be having qualms it should be his own parents. And himself!

They came round the side of the hut and looked inside.

The shock brought them up in their tracks.

Lying at the back, fast asleep, was a dark-skinned boy of about their own age. Stuck in the sand by his side, close to his outflung hand, was a dagger.

Chapter Four
Shiner Goes Under

WHAT HAD THEY expected? Some old fishermen with guns waiting for ducks to land? Certainly not what they found.

The boy lay on a dirty blanket full of holes. Apart from the blanket there was nothing else in the hut, no sign of food or water. The boy slept heavily. He had a fine hawked nose and dark, short curls falling untidily over his brow. The knife by his hand was large, curved and oriental-looking. And definitely designed for more than whittling sticks. Killing, Shiner thought. As they gazed at him, the boy stirred and muttered in his sleep and his hand moved to caress the knife. His eyes did not open.

Instinctively Corky and Shiner drew back from view round the side of the hut. They looked at each other. Shiner felt the hairs on the back of his neck stand up. It was so weird! They backed away, heading for their windsurfers. But their footprints were etched deeply in the sand.

"What on earth —"

Well away from the hut, they considered their options.

Corky said, "It all fits in with last night. Could be illegal immigrants. Dumped here from a boat from France. Or Holland. Picked up by someone this side."

"Why wasn't he moved out with the others last night?"

Corky shrugged. "Not enough room in the van? Hardly, he's not very big. Hasn't paid his dues? Perhaps he was only landed this morning. Going out tonight."

"He'll starve before long. Suppose they don't come back for him?"

"What shall we do?"

Shiner thought it wasn't for him to give the boy away. The boy had little enough chance without being informed on. What sort of a life was he fleeing from to make such a risky journey worthwhile? Or was he just in the hands of crooks?

As if answering the unspoken question, Corky said, "He's not a crook, after all. The crooks are the men who take in people like him and make them pay through the nose."

"We'll pretend we never saw him."

"Yeah."

"He'll know he's been seen though. By the footprints."

"We can't help that."

Shiner noticed that the wind had

come up since they had landed, but his head was so full of their strange experience that he set off from the island behind Corky without really noticing. It was only when Corky went whistling away ahead of him and the water started hitting him in the face that he realized that the conditions weren't very nice.

The wind was now against him, trying to take him back to the island, and the waves were considerably larger. The sun had disappeared behind huge mounds of grey cloud and the water looked dark and unkind. His head full of illegal immigrants, Shiner was not concentrating on the task in hand. He found that instead of following Corky, he was hardly leaving the island. How splendid was Corky's faith in him that he had disappeared almost out of sight!

Shiner tried to pull himself together. He had managed to launch successfully — not easy in the conditions. So where was his confidence? What's wrong with me? he wondered. He had scarcely made any way from the island and his board was zinging off in the wrong direction. All his expertise seemed to have vanished. It was essential to tack and change course else he would land up out at sea.

He unclipped his harness, moved his feet to put the board about and the next minute he was over and in the sea. He took in a huge mouthful of sea water and panicked. When he opened his mouth to scream he took in another dollop and his head went under. The water was freezing!

This was what he had dreaded. He was on his own with a vengeance, well out in a rough sea. He knew the technique of getting going, but it all seemed quite different with waves coming at him. On the smooth water of the reservoir it was no problem. Now, he was buffeted from all sides and couldn't breathe.

He couldn't shout either. Every time he opened his mouth to cough and choke, a wave slammed into his face and sent him under again. He knew he had to get his arms up over the board and hang on but somehow he couldn't get a grip. What was wrong with him?

Chapter Five
Abdul

WHAT WAS WRONG with him, he knew with certainty, was that he was drowning.

Shiner never knew whether he blanked out or not – perhaps more with fright than anything else – but eventually there was a voice shouting at him and suddenly, gloriously, ground under his feet! He stumbled, fell, got up again, blinking. Who was there, pulling him up out of the water?

He could not believe what had happened – that the wind and tide had driven him back on to the island. The boy pulling him out of the water was the one with the knife who had been asleep in the shed. The knife was now in a sheath on the boy's belt. He was talking but Shiner could not take in what he was saying. He pulled the board up out of the water. Shiner stumbled after him, trying to recover his breath.

The boy waited, muttering. A shout from seaward startled them and Corky came flying up to the beach, stopping with great panache just short of the shallow water and jumping off his board. His face was full of alarm.

"Holy Moses, Shiner! What are you up to?"

"Drowning."

"I thought you were right behind me, and then when I turned round – Jeez, nothing! What happened?"

"Nothing happened. I just fell over and couldn't get going."

Now the danger was over, the two boys realized they were involved with the boy they had so recently decided to leave in peace. The boy was pointing to their footsteps in the sand.

"Y-you . . . see me?"

"Yes," Corky said, shaking his head, "We won't tell."

He didn't seem to think Shiner falling in had been any great deal. He was already far more interested in trying to make out what the boy was trying to say than bothering about Shiner.

For this Shiner was relieved, thinking what an utter fool he had made of himself. Only what he had expected in the first place. But after the ride out, which had been so fantastic . . . what a blow, to lose it all so quickly! That was always the way. One moment everything went like clockwork, the next you were over and under and looking a prize jerk. Shiner was furious with himself.

Corky was making conversation with

the boy with gestures and basic English as if to an idiot. The boy looked puzzled, as well he might. Corky put his fingers to his lips in a shushing gesture and shook his head.

"No say. Us no say."

The boy said, "Abdul. My name is Abdul."

Corky blushed and said, "Sorry. My name's Corky and this is Shiner. What are you doing here?"

But Abdul didn't answer that one. Perhaps he didn't understand. Shiner rather thought he did.

He just said, "I wait." And sighed.

"You've got no food, no nothing."

"My friends come back tonight, to take me."

"Why didn't they take you with the others, last night?"

"You saw them last night?" The boy looked worried.

"Yes. We're living over there, on the point. We saw the van go past."

"They say nobody comes here. They are wrong then?"

"Well, we saw them."

"They take the others. But I go to a different place from the others. I go to my father who is here with political asylum. He is legal. But at home they try to take me, to get ransom money from my father. So I had to go – quickly – without permission. If I can get to my father all will be well."

"Where is your father?"

"Bradford."

"And if the police find you?"

"I will be put in prison while they examine my case. It takes months! You have to wait your turn. Wait, wait!"

Shiner began to think that living on the little island was quite a good alternative. Prison for months! While the sun was shining and the sea sparkled and people outside were hurrying and laughing and going about their ways. Even if they were sitting in the gutter, they were at least free. Shiner was appalled by the boy's plight.

"But they come tonight, to take me," he said.

"Are you sure?" Corky asked. What if they don't? both boys wondered.

Abdul shrugged, smiled. "I hope," he said.

Hope – was that all? Corky thought. Rather him than me! The boy was obviously intelligent and used to looking after himself.

"You tell no one," he said. Was it a question or an order?

"No, of course not." Corky hesitated, and said, "Are you hungry?"

"Very. Tonight my friends bring food. I wait."

Shiner didn't think he could be so calm under the same circumstances. He was still shaking from his fright coming off the board, and now realized that he had to face the same journey again. And get it right. Barely delivered from death, his problems were just as threatening as the stranded boy's. He had all the cares of the world on his shoulders. Get away — well, he'd tried once. But he had to. There was no alternative. The morning, from being all wonderful achievement and glory, had shattered into fragments.

"We'll be off then," Corky said to Abdul.

And to Shiner, "You'll make it this time, don't worry. Follow me. Do what I do. We'll make a long tack into shore and then tack again when we're quite close in. I won't go too close to the wind — free enough to make it easy. Just meet the waves as they come, at a slight angle is best. You can do it, no trouble."

Abdul helped Shiner off. He showed no emotion.

But Shiner had too much on his plate to worry about Abdul. Corky went off ahead of him, travelling far more slowly than before and turning round constantly to watch him. Shiner fiddled his feet into the best position and concentrated on getting his balance right.

First time out he hadn't been concentrating. Now he concentrated with all his being, spurred by the horrors he had just experienced. To his relief he seemed to get it right this time. He managed to hit the waves at the right angle, learning all the time. Get it right and swoosh down the other side . . .

fantastic! Once more, confidence crept back. Corky was close to him. He only had to do what Corky did.

The buoy they had passed on the way out was quite close. It now sat on a sandbank. No wonder Corky had said avoid it. Strange that way out here, still well off land, the water shallowed to ankle height.

They had to go about to avoid the sandbank but this time Shiner turned perfectly. For heaven's sake, he had done it often enough at home! But still the nervous tension gripped him. He now knew that getting it right out here could be a matter of life and death. But the knowledge made the whole thing far more exciting. Whether he liked this tingling feeling of half terror, half pure joy, he could not decide. When he reached land, he would know.

Not making another mistake, he saw the land drawing steadily closer. It might be boring for Corky, but for himself –

"Fantastic! Terrific!"

He almost burst into tears of joy as he stepped off the board on to the little shell beach. The relief overwhelmed him. It was all he could do not to drop down on his knees and kiss the ground.

Corky was laughing. "Said you could do it!"

"You'd have been back hours ago," Shiner said admiringly. He could see how brilliant Corky was.

Even more brilliant not to swank

about it. To be patient with a loser like Shiner. That was true friendship, not to be patronizing.

In the pleasure and gratification of having done something really good, they both forgot about Abdul. They hid the boards in the dunes, covering them with sand and grass, then set off to bike home. But as they rode, they remembered the boy's lonely plight. They turned and stared back at the island. It looked very small in the mass of empty foam-flicked water. It was cold now. Abdul had only the thin blanket, cotton clothes, no food, no water. What if the motor boat didn't come back for him?

"Should we worry about him, do you think?"

"That boat'll come for him tonight, bet you. We'll hear the van go past."

"Yes! We'll listen for it. And then we'll know he's safe."

"Safeish," said Corky.

"It's bound to come for him. They wouldn't just leave him?"

"No. They wouldn't just leave him."

But somehow, they both thought they might.

Chapter Six
To the Rescue

"I don't know what's the matter with you two tonight. You're like a couple of cats on hot bricks."

Trying to listen for the Transit van, or catch sight of a light down the lane, Corky kept wandering over to the window, fingering the curtains. Shiner kept going to the door saying he could hear a cat.

Dr North was playing Wagner on the CD-player and they couldn't hear a thing outside. A fire was lit in the old-fashioned hearth and softly shaded lamps made the room cosy and comforting. Mrs North was doing her tapestry — a cushion cover with a unicorn on it and daisies on the grass. It was a setting of peace and comfort. But both boys could not stop thinking about the boy on the island.

"It's freezing out there," Shiner whispered to Corky.

They were both full of roast pork and roast potatoes and peas and they kept thinking about Abdul. They thought the van would come and they could forget the whole thing. To be on that island now, in the dark, the waves lapping softly on the cold sand – abandoned – it didn't bear thinking about. But the van didn't come.

They went up to their room so that they could mount a vigil in the window.

"What if it doesn't come?"

"It's bound to come."

"Shall we tell your parents?"

"No!"

"Why not?"

Corky didn't answer. There were so many reasons! First, he wasn't supposed to go as far as the island. His father would be furious that he had taken Shiner there. Even Corky now realized what a risk they had taken. (But Shiner had his head screwed on the right way – he had been great.)

Also his father would be really angry if he had to raise the police and get involved in a great kerfuffle. He came on holiday for peace and quiet. Also – mostly – something about Abdul and his bravery gave Corky a desperate desire to help him. If they told the police, he would go to prison. He had been quick enough to help Shiner when Shiner needed it. Now it was their turn to help him.

"If the van doesn't come, we'll have to do something," Shiner said. "We can't just leave him there to starve. We're the only ones who know he's there."

"Yes, I know," Corky said crossly.

"Why don't we tell your parents?" Shiner said again.

To Shiner it was the easy solution, shift the burden on to someone responsible.

"We might have to. But shut up about it."

Up in the attic room they mounted a vigil at the window. Outside the grass was stiffening with frost, the sky was glittering with cold stars. No light showed.

"Well, they'll leave it till two or three o'clock in the morning," Corky said, "so's not to get caught."

They decided to stay awake in turns,

first Shiner, then Corky, until the van came.

It was terribly difficult. First they had to set the alarm clock and then make sure the parents wouldn't hear it. Corky put it under his pillow. Shiner sat by the window watching but his eyes kept closing. He told himself he was bound to wake if the van came, as it had to pass so close to the bungalow.

Corky's parents listened to music until nearly midnight, then went to bed. Their bedroom was downstairs, which helped. Shiner sat on, and gave over to Corky at two o'clock. Corky fetched his sleeping bag and sat huddled in the window. Shiner went back to bed but now, perversely, could not sleep.

By the time morning came neither of them had seen nor heard the van, and they both felt they hadn't slept at all.

The doctor and his wife were full of spirits and laughed at the boys' bleary faces.

"What time did you put the light out? Dawn, by the look of you! You'll have to take a nap this afternoon like a couple of poor old grandpas! We're off to play golf today. You can come if you like and do the putting course while we play."

"No fear. We'd rather mess about here."

"All right. There's plenty of food in the fridge. There's cold pork and you can make some chips. And there's an apple pie. Help yourselves. Do you want anything? We'll be passing the shops."

"A new sail," Corky said.

His mother laughed. "You'll be lucky! I meant toothpaste, chocolate, that sort of thing."

Shiner thought: yes. Help.

But Corky stubbornly said nothing.

It seemed to take the parents ages to set off. When they finally left both boys knew they had to sort out their problem first, before they did anything else.

"We'll take him some food," Corky decided. "Then we can think about it without feeling he's dying of starvation while we're dithering about here. We can ask him what he wants us to do."

They took a load of food out of the

fridge and some cans of drink and packed it in Corky's rucksack. They found a spare blanket in the wardrobe in their bedroom and Corky stuffed that in too.

"You can take it out there. Wind it round your middle under your belt. And don't fall in."

Shiner realized that Corky took it for granted that he was coming too. The morning was cold but sunny, the wind steady, not too strong. But big cumulus clouds were gathering on the horizon. The fact that Corky took it for granted that Shiner was coming made Shiner feel more confident. Corky obviously was not afraid for him. So why should he be afraid for himself? Shiner smiled to himself at the puzzle.

They cycled down to the beach to where they had left their boards hidden in the dunes. Shiner was more worried for Abdul than he was for himself this time. Suppose he had died in the cold? What if they landed on the island and there was a dead body waiting for them? What would Corky do then? Mount a funeral service probably. Sew the body up in a sack and put it out to sea.

Shiner's heart lurched with fear. Some holiday this was turning out to be! The blanket round his middle was a real bind, literally, hampering his ability on the board. But Corky was no better off with the rucksack.

"All set?" Corky was ready to go.

"Yes. OK."

"I'll keep close."

Once again the island looked miles away. But it was astonishing how fast a board could cover the distance. The record for speed was just under fifty miles an hour! Shiner thought of this as he felt the wind take a hold and the board lift under his feet.

Now, suddenly, he didn't feel afraid any more. The strength of the wind was something to play with – give in to it, use it to the best of his ability. See the squalls coming as they raced across the water under the shadow of the big clouds and be ready for the yank of the boom in his hands. It was terrific!

The reservoir now seemed the dullest

playground in the world with its flat surface and concrete walls. The spray stung his face. His adventures of the day before seemed to have given him a new expertise. He had overcome conditions that he wouldn't have dreamed of venturing out in without Corky's encouragement. His instructor had been telling him for weeks that he could do it, if he would just believe in himself. Now he did.

Chapter Seven
Trouble

THE ISLAND CAME gradually nearer. Corky kept close, whizzing backwards and forwards at great speed, enjoying himself. Shiner kept on his course steadily. With Corky watching him, he felt confident and happy. He had to tack several times as the wind was mostly against them, but he had no trouble.

The trouble lay ahead.

They could make out Abdul watching them from the beach. Shiner had to land without getting the blanket wet. But he managed beautifully. Corky was waiting to help, but he didn't need help. He jumped off knee-deep and they pulled up the board. What a difference from last time! Corky shrugged out of the rucksack and dropped it on the sand.

"For you," he said to the boy. "Food."

Abdul's eyes gleamed. He looked haggard and was shivering in spite of having the blanket wrapped round him.

"They didn't come for me!" He didn't

sound as confident as he had the day before. In fact his voice choked. But then, strongly, "They will tonight. They must!"

He drank down a whole can of orange juice and tore into a meat pie like a ravening wolf. Corky and Shiner were impressed. Then it occurred to them that they got hungry even between three large meals a day and were forever snacking out of the fridge. Abdul had been without food for two whole nights and a day and a half! No wonder. The second can of orange juice was gone, and all the cherry cake.

When he was beginning to slow down a bit, Corky said, "Why didn't they come? Will they come tonight?"

"I don't know," Abdul said. Then he

shook his head. "They are very bad men. I do not like depending on them. But it was the only way."

"They run a racket?"

Abdul looked confused.

"Bringing in illegal immigrants for money?" Corky explained.

"Yes. They are very greedy. Some people die – in the holds of the ships. It happens. And those men, they still take the money. They are very wicked."

"They wouldn't leave you here, surely?"

Abdul shrugged. "They might. They've already got my money."

Corky said – what else could he say? – "If they don't come, we'll make sure you're rescued."

"If I'm rescued, I'll be taken to the police."

"Not if we rescue you," Corky said.

Shiner didn't see how they could. Perhaps Corky knew someone with a boat, who could be trusted.

But just as he was going to ask him, Abdul gave a shout and pointed across to the far side of the island. Not very far away, approaching fast, was a large, tatty-looking motor boat.

"They're here! They've come to fetch me!" The relief on his face was evident.

Then, immediately, he saw the danger. So did Corky.

"I think we should get out of here! And fast!"

"Yes," said Abdul. "It's best they don't see you."

Best, perhaps, but impossible. The motor boat was throttling down. The boys could see three men on the bow. They looked nasty.

"I don't think I want to meet them. Goodbye, Abdul, nice knowing you!"

And Corky tore off down the beach towards the stranded boards, Shiner at his heels.

Chapter Eight
"I can't go any faster!"

THERE WAS NO time to think. No way
did they want to be caught. The men in
the boat were unlikely to take kindly to
having their illegal business discovered.
Probably take them off to sea and chuck
them overboard, Shiner thought. If they

were thoughtful enough to throw their boards in as well, no one would suppose their deaths were other than a sad accident.

"Jeez, let's not get caught!" Corky muttered, thinking along the same lines.

They gathered up their boards and waded out into the water. The wind had come up once more and was blowing quite strongly. It would be on the beam for heading home, the best place for fast travelling — not against them like yesterday.

Spurred by necessity, Shiner made a brilliant launch. Corky creamed beside him, pale-faced.

"Don't look now," he said, "but I think they're coming after us."

Shiner nearly fell off his board.

"They've not dropped anchor. They're revving up and putting out into deep water again."

Shiner daren't look in case he lost his balance. Trying to sail as fast as Corky was using all his attention.

"What are they going to do?" he squeaked.

"Sink us if they can. You've got to move, Shiner."

"I can't go any faster!"

"Get your weight forward a bit. Bend your knees more."

Beside him, Corky's board was planing, carving a frothing, seething wake. Corky looked effortless on top, turning to watch the intentions of the motor boat.

"Yes, coming round the island. Opening the throttle."

"Will they catch us?"

"Sounds a ropy motor to me. Depends on its horsepower. We can make a lot of knots, Shiner, if you try your best."

Shiner was already going faster than he had ever gone in his life. The board surged and leapt under his feet, breasting the waves, throwing up sheets of spray. And now, although he was frightened of his pursuers, he was no longer frightened of what he was doing. It was terrific! He had learnt what windsurfing was all about in the last two days. Learnt what he was capable of. His instructor would be proud of him!

Just as well.

Corky shouted. "They're after us all right. Gaining a tiny bit – not much though! Just keep it up, Shiner. We'll do it!"

Was Corky just spurring him on with his encouragement? A snatched glance behind showed him the motor boat clear of the island now, heading their way. Its bow was high and menacing. A figure stood there, shouting instructions.

He daren't look again! Just trim the board, free off a little. The board leapt and shuddered under his feet as if it were alive. And Shiner felt as if he had come alive too, after a year of sleep, the adrenalin flowing. He felt electric. He knew he was grinning all over his face! It was crazy.

But Corky was coming alongside.

"They're catching up!" he shouted.

Shiner bit his lip. What else to do? Corky was flying. If only he could go as fast! But strive as he might, he couldn't get the performance that Corky could. And it mattered. Jeez, how it mattered! It mattered life and death. Shiner's manic excitement hardened into fear. He could hear the steady noise of the launch's engine behind him, coming and going on the wind but never receding. Gradually, slowly, getting nearer. It was unrelenting. Terrifying.

Shiner had never thought about death before. It wasn't something that had ever bothered him. But he did now. Being pushed over, prodded under. Hit on the head. Go faster, board! He prayed, gibbered, near to sobbing. But concentrating all the time, hitting the waves square, hurtling down the long troughs . . . the shore seemed as far away as ever.

Corky came flying up alongside. Shouting something.

"What?"

"Make for the buoy!"

The buoy was just about on course, but still far away. Beyond, impossibly far, a shaft of sunlight caught the dunes, serene in the morning. Corky's parents were playing golf, laughing and talking. Shiner felt he was in a dream. Or a nightmare.

Corky was still shouting something.

"Put them aground! If we're lucky . . ."

Of course! The buoy marked the shoal, but these strangers wouldn't know that, with luck. It was their only chance, Shiner could see. Another quick glance behind showed the motor boat definitely gaining.

The awful thing was, Shiner was sure Corky could keep ahead without any trouble. But he was trimming his speed to keep with him, Shiner. Shiner kept his eyes on his sail, trying his hardest to use the wind. Forget the pursuit.

But now he could hear the rough grinding of the launch's engine behind him. Voices shouting. It was clear they were going to try and run them down. The man on the bow now had a boat-hook in his hand.

Corky's face was white.

"Go for it, Shiner!"

The buoy bobbed on the water ahead, not so far away now. There was no sand showing, but it must be very close to the surface. This time yesterday it was showing. The tide came high an hour later every day. Corky was heading straight for it.

"Will the boards clear it?" Shiner shouted.

"They've got to!" Corky shouted back.

It was their only chance. As his board flew over the waves Shiner could hear agitated shouting from behind. He just hoped it didn't mean they knew what the buoy meant. But no, they were not altering course. The buoy was coming up fast and so was the motor launch.

Corky swooped beside him. "Start praying!" And he laughed.

Was he so sure? Shiner never knew. He just knew that in a trough, suddenly, he could see sand below him. His board breasted the next wave and swooshed down the far side. At the same time there was a shriek from behind. A violent roaring of the motor, a grinding noise. Furious shouts.

The boat had been travelling fast and went aground hard. The tide was falling rapidly. The people on board obviously had no knowledge of shoal waters, and hadn't the sense to put the engine in reverse immediately. That might have got them off. But they didn't even realize what had happened. They thought they had hit a wreck or some sort of obstruction. The boys could tell by the way they ran round the deck shouting and peering. By the time they realized what had happened and revved up the engine in reverse, it was too late. They were well and truly hard aground.

Shiner nearly fell over with sheer relief.

Corky was almost dancing on his board, laughing and shrieking.

"We've got 'em! We've done it!"

He came skimming across Shiner's

wake. "We're off the hook! In the clear! Alive, man!"

Afterwards, Shiner realized what a close call it had been. Another hundred metres and the man with the boat-hook would have got him. What a perfect murder too! No witnesses. No questions asked. Two boys too far out. Foolhardy. Unsupervised.

The relief had him almost crying. The board seemed to be doing its own thing without him, skipping shoreward like a dolphin with him a zombie on top. His arms ached and his legs felt like water. But he couldn't fall over now. They were in deep water again and the tops of the waves curled white. He felt really whacked.

At last the dunes were opening their soft, sandy arms towards the skimming sails. The clouds made great running shadows along the shore. It was glorious.

Corky rode towards him, getting ready to land.

"What next?" he said.

Shiner hadn't thought about that.

Chapter Nine
The Only Chance for Abdul

THEY BOTH FLOPPED down on the sand beside the boards. Shiner could feel himself shaking all over, but wasn't sure if Corky was. The relief of being on solid ground was phenomenal – and not being dead.

They were for real, those crooks.

Out at sea, all was peaceful. Nothing looked out of place. Only the old motor launch sat skewed, drying out now on the sandbank that appeared to have risen from nowhere. Several men could be seen clambering anxiously around the tilting deck.

On this coast sailors often went aground. Only the locals knew how to find their way through the ever-shifting shoals. These men were strangers, amazed that they could be in shallow water so far from the shore.

They were too far offshore for swimming to be an option – the deep water on the shore side was almost a mile wide. They were stuck there until the next high water, when the tide would float them off.

"There's no hurry," Corky said.

They lay in the sun for a while, recovering. It seemed incredibly peaceful, with only the soft rustle of the wind in the stiff marram grass and the distant cries of gulls out at sea. No wonder the doctor came here to unwind!

Neither of the boys said how they had felt. There was no need really. Only, "We were lucky," Corky said solemnly.

Then he said, "Thought you said you were no good?" and grinned.

"I've never done it before. Not like that. Not on the reservoir. If you didn't think you were going to die . . . it's brilliant."

"Going for your life. Really."

"Yeah, great." And they both laughed.

After the adrenalin started to cool, they realized that they had landed themselves with dire responsibilities. They had captured a bunch of crooks single-handed. Great. Big deal. They had only to ring the police and get them captured.

But what about Abdul? He would be rounded up too.

The crooks wouldn't be able to move until the tide came back to float them off, which would take twelve hours.

"We could rescue Abdul before we ring the police," Corky said. "There's plenty of time."

"How? We haven't got a boat."

Corky said, "On the board."

"*What?*"

Shiner couldn't believe what he was hearing.

"People do it, if there's been an accident or something."

"Have you ever done it?"

"No."

"You can't! It's too . . . too risky!" Not to mention crazy, he thought.

"Yeah, but what else can we do? We go and get help for Abdul and he'll be taken to the police. And getting help will take hours from here. By the time we get back with a boat the crooks'll be afloat again. But if we nip out now – we'll get Abdul out and away."

"We?" quavered Shiner.

"I'll fetch him but I'll have to use

your board. It's better for the job. And you can come out on mine, in case there's a problem."

Shiner felt himself panicking. In case there was a problem? If he went on Corky's board there would be a problem all right.

He tried to put this into words.

But Corky actually laughed. "*You* are the problem, Shiner — not believing in yourself. Of course you can cope with my board. I *need* you with me, don't you see? Anything might happen and two of us are better than one."

Anything might happen . . . Shiner tried to beat down the panic. Corky was just saying how good he was to jolly him along.

"But your board . . . I wouldn't . . ."

"My board is actually easier. It's faster, you wait till you try it!" Corky jumped up, obviously not doubting that Shiner was going to agree to the plan. Corky was a man of action. Having thought up the plan, he was ready to go.

"You can see it's the only chance for Abdul," he said.

Shiner wanted to suggest that he stay where he was and watch Corky carry out this rescue, but the words died on his tongue. Corky would know he was chicken then. He *was* chicken. But this was his chance to . . . to what? Die? Prove himself? Impress Corky? No. The real answer was: impress himself. Corky assumed he could do it, just as his instructor had. Why did it take so much effort for him to believe the same?

"OK," he said.

"We'll fetch him, get him off to Bradford or wherever, and then ring the police and tell them about the boat aground, and the van we heard going up the lane in the night. No one need ever know about Abdul."

"OK." No fuss. Fight down the panic. Of course he could do it.

"Do you want to take my board now? Get the hang of it on the way out? You'll really see the difference. You'll love it, Shiner! Come on!"

Corky was off, all bounce again. And yet what he was intending to do was really hairy, Shiner knew.

Shiner pretended it was a lesson, like on the reservoir. Trying out a new board. He shut his eyes to the far horizon, pretended there were concrete banks all round him. It was all in the mind. Up and away.

He waded out with Corky's board. The wind was perfect, steady, not gusting, and fairly brisk. The sea was smooth, the wind blowing over the outgoing tide, not against it. He could do it. Only half an hour ago he had been laughing with the fun of it – on his own board.

Corky was ahead as usual, already on his way. The heavy board flew for Corky, just as Shiner knew it would. And before he realized it, he was catching up! He wasn't doing anything any different, but he was certainly travelling. He couldn't believe it.

"What did I tell you?" Corky shouted. "Piece of cake, isn't it?"

Shiner knew, in the conditions, he had no excuse for falling off, and the feel of it filled him with wonder – it was magic! Flying! After the first few minutes of standing like a petrified zombie, the movement under his feet compelled him to start adjusting his weight to the pull of the sail – surfing like a real pro. How delicate was the balance after the heavy board! It made him rise to it, it brought out the skill he could never convince himself he possessed.

Corky was alongside, laughing. And already they were passing the grounded launch, but well out of range, just in case. Four men were watching them from the cockpit. It was great to see their frustration. Shiner really believed they had intended to drown them less than an hour before. He wished he could spare a hand to wave, but decided against it.

This trip Shiner kept up easily with Corky, and they came in to the island together. Abdul was waiting for them on the beach, anxious and inquiring.

He could not understand that he was being offered a trip to land.

"How?"

Corky explained. Watching Abdul's face, it was a comfort for Shiner to know that he wasn't the only one frightened by Corky's fearless plans. He found he was joining with Corky in trying to persuade Abdul it was nothing to be afraid of, and at the same time he almost laughed aloud listening to himself – what a mixed-up twit he was!

"It's your only chance to get away, don't you see?" Corky implored him.

"They tried to catch you! I thought they were going to kill you!"

"Yes, so did we, mate. They're no good, that lot."

"They might come back for me."

"And they might not." Better not say he and Corky intended to shop them to the police.

"Come on, it's your best chance. Trust

us. We'll see you on your way to Bradford."

"I've got no money!"

"We've got some," Corky said grandly.

"I can't swim."

"You aren't going to swim."

"I'm frightened!"

Shiner felt a lurch of compassion for the boy. He knew how he felt all right – but on top of that Abdul was in an alien country, bereft of friends, and in danger from the police.

Shiner said, "We were frightened, the last trip. When the boat chased us."

Abdul nodded.

"This isn't as dangerous as our last trip. Corky knows what he's doing."

Abdul fell silent, and the boys guessed their persuasion was working. It wasn't hard for him to see, after the first fright, that it was true he didn't have much choice.

"All you've got to do", said Corky, "is sit up front and hold on to the mast. Nothing else. I do the rest."

Shiner felt a churning in his stomach. What if Corky went over? What on earth was he expected to do? Don't think about it.

"All right?" Corky was jigging with impatience.

"Yes. I'll come."

"Great! Let's go!"

They pulled the boards out into the water. Abdul was told where to sit. He

95

clutched the mast like a drowning man. Corky launched carefully, freeing off to get going, and Shiner followed.

Shiner found he was concentrating so much on watching Corky that he made his launch instinctively. It was as different from the last time off the island as it was possible to be. He was up and travelling, and not even thinking about it.

All his fears were for Corky, now riding a very heavy and lumbersome board in a wind that was inconveniently dropping off. Shiner's problem was to stay with him, not go tearing off ahead. Corky wasn't laughing now, but frowning up into his sail, making minute adjustments to the wind.

It occurred to Shiner then that Corky

had far more reason to be frightened than he did.

He found he was tacking backwards and forwards to keep with him, and not even thinking about getting it wrong. He was concentrating on Corky's problems. Corky had to tack too and with Abdul at the mast it wasn't easy. But Corky's skill prevailed. Slowly they made towards the shore, well clear of the grounded launch.

Shiner was just beginning to realize how fantastic the whole exercise was proving, when an unfamiliar sound came to his ears. An engine.

A glance round showed nothing on the sea. But from away over the peninsula a little white bird glinted in the sky. A helicopter. Coming their way. He zoomed in close to Corky and shouted at him.

Corky shouted back, "White! That's the police!"

Shiner's heart sank. Was their rescue going to be in vain?

The afternoon was drawing on and their sails cast long shadows across the golden sea as they surfed towards the shore. Two boys out enjoying themselves – why should the helicopter think otherwise?

Surely, after all this, they weren't going to fail?

Chapter Ten
No Going Back

THEY FLOUNDERED UP the beach.

Corky hissed to Abdul, "Run up into the dunes and hide yourself in the grass. Quickly! So they don't see you."

He jabbed his finger to point to the helicopter. It was still some way over the land, obviously heading for the grounded launch. Would they notice the antics of the boys on the beach?

Abdul darted off.

Corky and Shiner turned to dismantling the boards as if they were just in from a harmless spin. Shiner could feel his heart pounding uncomfortably. The helicopter came over the end of the point, not exactly overhead but pretty near.

Corky and Shiner could see the pilot looking down on them. They carried on tidying up the boards as if nothing was out of the ordinary, praying that Abdul had hidden himself well. The pilot made no sign, but turned to stare ahead at the motor boat.

"I'm sure it's the police," Corky said. "They're circling."

The helicopter went no further than the stranded launch. It circled round it and hovered over it for some time. The men had all disappeared below.

"It can't land on the sandbank. There's not enough room," Corky said.

"I bet they'd like to."

"They can radio for help if they want it. They might bring a police launch in."

"Well, I hope they shove off so Abdul can get out." Shiner rather wanted to get out too. He felt he had had enough adventure for one day.

But the helicopter made no move to depart. It hovered offshore for some minutes, quite low over the launch.

Then it heaved itself up high and swung away.

Then —

"It's coming back," Corky squawked.

They thought it would fly away, but to their horror it came back straight for the point of the shore where they had beached, hovered for a minute or two, blowing sand all over them, then settled down to land. The noise and blast of air from the rotor nearly knocked them over.

Shiner thought they must have seen Abdul hiding.

The engine was turned off and the silence that followed seemed as shattering as the racket. One of the men — the passenger — climbed down and walked slowly across to the dunes. He climbed up and looked all round.

Shiner felt himself freezing with apprehension. Their bikes lay there, and Abdul. How well had Abdul hidden? The two boys tried to go naturally about the business of dismantling their boards, but Shiner knew that Corky's heart was hammering as nervously as his own.

But the man made no exclamations of discovery. He sauntered back and asked, "Those your bikes?"

"Yes."

"You live near here?"

Corky told him.

"Did you see that boat go aground?"

"Yes, we did."

"D'you know who they are?"

"No. We saw them close to and we'd never seen them before."

The man introduced himself as a police officer. It was hard to know how much to tell him, knowing Abdul was hiding close by. Shiner left it to Corky, and Corky told him about the van coming up the lane two nights ago. He didn't say anything about going out to the island, or being chased by the launch. The man took some notes, and then wandered off and talked into a mobile phone. Then, after taking the boys' address, he got back into the helicopter.

Corky and Shiner watched it start up and take off.

"I wouldn't mind a ride in one of

104

those. Must get a fantastic view," Corky said.

"Quicker to Bradford than a bike," Shiner said.

"He must have hidden himself well. They never saw him."

He had. They didn't see him either until some sand stirred in the bottom of one of the dips. A dusty figure sat up, shaking a clump of marram grass from his head.

"Abdul!"

"It is safe now?"

"Yes, they've gone. But let's get a move on. I think they'll be back."

Two bikes between three was not ideal but Abdul wasn't heavy. They shared giving him a lift home, sitting him on the crossbar. Corky had been planning to get his money, give it to Abdul and cycle with him to the nearest town and bus station. (He thought his father might kindly refund the money if he told him later what had happened . . . he hoped.) But when they got near the bungalow they saw the car parked in front of it and realized that the parents were already home.

"Jeez!" Corky braked so hard that Shiner ran into the back of him. Abdul was sitting on Shiner's crossbar and shot off into the road.

"What is it?"

Shiner's heart sank. So much had been going on that they hadn't realized the afternoon had already turned into evening and the sun was just about to depart behind the flat fields to the west. He could see Mrs North moving about in the kitchen.

Corky dropped his bike, grabbed Abdul by the arm and ran with him to the ramshackle garden shed round the side of the house. He kicked open the door and shoved him inside. It was mostly full of an ancient lawnmower and some old garden chairs.

"Stay here! We don't want them to see you!"

He slammed the door on Abdul's startled face.

"Now what?" Shiner squeaked. (Would these shocks never end?)

Corky groaned. "Trust them to be

early tonight! We'll have to see what happens. Might be a chance to get away after supper."

Shiner felt he had lost all track of time. He felt really tired. His arms and shoulders were aching. The thought of a good supper, a hot bath and bed was tempting. But he was pretty sure it wasn't going to happen.

How right he was!

Supper was quick. Mrs North had it on the table five minutes after they got in. Tucking in, they both thought of poor Abdul, supperless in the garden shed. But there was no way of saving any. It was all runny – stew with gravy and peas followed by ice cream, which was eaten right up. Oh, for slumping down in front of the box!

"When they start playing their old opera stuff we can go upstairs and out of the window, down the roof and away," Corky said.

"Away to where? Bradford?"

"No, twit. Just get him on his way. Out of the danger area."

Shiner thought it would be them in the danger area if Ma and Pa North found out what was going on.

They nobly wiped up the supper things. Then, just as they were finishing, Mrs North said to Corky, "I want you to write your thank-you letters tonight. Your birthday was a fortnight ago and you still haven't done them. You had money from both lots of grandparents, and really nice things from Auntie Peggy and Auntie Maureen and it's high time you wrote those letters."

"But, Mum, I can do them tomorrow. Shiner and I are going to —"

"I don't care what you've planned, dear. You've put it off for too long. Why should your relatives bother to remember you if you can't spare five minutes to write them a letter? Especially Granny and Grandpa — you know how they like to hear from you. When you're old you'll remember . . ." Etc., etc., etc.

Shiner's heart sank. He knew Corky was truly caught. Four letters at least!

"It'll take me all night!" Corky

breathed at Shiner. "When she says write a letter she really means it! Not just 'thank you, love Corky.'"

"It's all right. I'll sort Abdul," Shiner said.

As he said it, he almost thought they would all notice his hair rising up and standing on end. What was he doing? He, Shiner, who always followed the others, who always played the waiting game to see how the land lay was now casually tossing off this promise as if he ran a professional firm for harbouring criminals. He could scarcely believe his own voice.

Corky looked at him keenly. The surprise in his face was plain.

"You mean it?"

"Yes." Not even a tremor in his voice! Firm and resolute.

"Wow, that's great, Shiner!" There was real respect in Corky's voice. "It will make it much safer. I can cover up for you if you don't get back."

Safer for who? Shiner's inner voice cried. "If you don't get back . . ." What did he mean by that? Shiner felt his lips tremble. But he'd jumped in with both big feet – no going back now.

Chapter Eleven
"Just surfing around"

AFTERWARDS, HE SUPPOSED that what
he had achieved that day had given him
this rare courage. He was acting in his
new character. Shiner the Super Surfer!
The new confidence had prompted him
to speak out.

Now, he was not so sure.

He was even less sure when he was outside in the dark, making for the garden shed. He had Corky's savings in his pocket. Corky's parents thought he was having an early night, worn out with surfing.

"Abdul!"

Cautiously he pulled open the shed door.

Abdul was sitting in a garden chair.

"We can go now. It's all clear. I've got some money for you."

"To Bradford?"

Shiner nodded hopefully. He wasn't sure where Bradford was, but small things like that mustn't put him off. It was like surfing – go for it. Hit the big

114

wave smack on.

At least there was a bike each now. It made life easier. Abdul was very cheerful. It struck Shiner that being off the island would make anyone feel better. The loneliness out there must have been dreadful.

All was dark and quiet out at sea, although it was too early yet for the tide to have come up and floated the launch. The evening was calm and stars filled the cloudless sky. Two boys cycling into town would not attract anyone's notice. The bikes had lights and all was in order.

The nearest town was five miles away and it felt like ten. On the outskirts they came to a supermarket, still open. With a flash of inspiration, Shiner went in and found a motoring map, and looked up Bradford.

He showed it to Abdul, and Abdul memorized the towns he must make for to get there. To be on the safe side Shiner picked up a felt marking pen and wrote them on Abdul's arm. He put the map and the pen back — no one had noticed — and they went back to the bikes and cycled to the bus station.

There was a police car parked at the entrance.

Shiner stopped, feeling his heart begin to thump. They pulled the bikes up on to the pavement and pretended to be looking in a shop window. It was full of sweets and toys, rather babyish stuff. Shiner found he was staring at Barbie dolls and stuffed elephants.

A policeman came out of the shop. He had a packet of cigarettes in his hand. He got into the car and drove away.

Shiner laughed. They locked the bikes to a lamp-post and went to study the buses. Abdul looked at the towns on his arm, and found one which was marked on the front of a bus. It was due to go in ten minutes.

"You'll be on your way. First stop."

Shiner handed over the money, and showed Abdul the note he thought would cover the first leg. He went back to the sweet shop and bought some chocolate bars and stuffed them in

Abdul's pocket. And a can of drink. What else?

He couldn't think of anything. They went back to the bus. Several people were now on board and the driver was coming out of the shelter.

"You go now," Shiner said.

Abdul grinned.

Shiner felt a funny sort of sadness. Having done so much, he now felt he was leaving Abdul in the lurch. The great adventure for Abdul was just starting. For him, Shiner, it was over. He could do no more.

As the bus swung away out into the road, Shiner saw Abdul's nose pressed to the window, the great dark eyes staring out in excitement. With him went

Corky's hard-won savings. Corky would never receive a thank-you letter. What a strange day!

Was it worth it?

Cycling home, Shiner had time to reflect. Plenty of time, in fact, for riding one bike and guiding the other was slow and difficult. After all the frights, he felt he had come out on top. The further his tired legs took him, the deeper grew the satisfaction. He had not failed. Even in this last test – finding the towns for Abdul, finding the bus station – it had come out all right. Corky had doubted him. He could remember Corky's expression: the surprise. But he had surprised himself too. Shiner was happy.

When he got home he remembered he was supposed to be in bed. Luckily the old opera was blaring out in the living room, so no one heard him climbing up the roof into the bedroom window. Then, quite unable to sleep, he put his pyjamas on and went downstairs. He would say he wanted a drink.

He opened the living-room door, nearly colliding with Corky who was just coming to bed. He had time to whisper, "All's well. He caught a bus," before Mrs North remarked, "My word, you look as if you've just come in from sailing, Shiner! I thought you wanted an early night?"

Shiner faked a great yawn. "I'm really thirsty. Want a —" yawn — "drink."

"Yes, I put too much salt in the potatoes. That's what's made you thirsty." She turned the opera down and switched on the television instead. "We'll just watch the news. Then I think we're all ready for bed."

Shiner got a glassful of water and sat down on the sofa. A mistake. He nearly fell asleep before he'd drunk the water. But on the television the newscaster was talking about a boat-load of crooks being rounded up by the inshore police-boat ". . . a gang wanted for running a trade in illegal immigrants from Holland. Their boat went aground off the Flatlands shore this afternoon."

"Well I never," said Mrs North, "on our doorstep! What were you boys doing all day, with this going on under your nose?"

Corky yawned. "Nothing much."

Shiner yawned too. "Just surfing around," he said.

They yawned together.

"Nothing really."